The Unlikely Adventure
of a Turtle, a Mouse and a Shark

by Lyn Wells Clark

illustrated by
Lorena Mary Hart

SHAYLANE,

ENJOY THE ADVENTURE!

LYN WELLS CLARK

Much love and gratitude
to my wonderful family!

Thank you for believing in me, pushing me
and inspiring me to fulfill my dream!
This would not have happened
without your love and support!

The Unlikely Adventure of a Turtle, a Mouse and a Shark
by Lyn Wells Clark

Published by Blue-Eyed Star Creations, LLC and Carolyn Clark
2 Old Forest St.
Middleton, MA 01949

blue-eyedstarcreations.com

Illustrations by Lorena Mary Hart © Blue-Eyed Star Creations, LLC and Carolyn Clark

ISBN: 978-0-99944-090-2

This book is dedicated to my three blue-eyed stars in the heavens:

John "Turtle" Doherty,
Joe "Mousie" Doherty,
Michael "Jaws" Doherty

I carry you in my heart every day!

There is a brotherhood of blue-eyed stars
that protects the heavens, always on guard.
They serve Queen Celestia with great pride
sworn to obey, and faithfully abide.

One day they found a traitor in their ranks—
a beloved servant at the Queen's right flank.
He was one of her most trusted soldiers,
but his greedy heart grew colder and colder.

He was cast aside when he led an attack;
his light turned out, his eyes turned black.
He betrayed his brothers to attain great power,
but the Dark Star was defeated in his darkest hour.

Now he awaits each lunar eclipse,
to reduce the celestial army with every trip.
Darkness is his cover as he slips into position.
Take them one by one: this is his mission.

Three stars would fall on this fateful night.
The brothers were ambushed in the vanishing moonlight.
In the ink-colored sky the three were cursed,
and when the spell was cast, they fell to earth.

"You will never find each other, of that I am sure,
and for this curse, that is the only cure,"
the Dark Star snorted as he cast the spell.
Then one by one, the brothers fell.

The first found himself underground,
with tiny creatures and tunnels all around.
They had pointy ears and skinny tails.
They scampered about, in and out of their trails.

The other mice couldn't help but notice
the striking blue eyes that were now their focus.
"Where are you from?" one of the elders asked.
The brother told him of the spell that was cast.

"I must find my brothers and break the curse,
but they could be anywhere on this earth."
The elder replied, "Seek the one who seeks you.
Find a pair of eyes of sparkling blue."

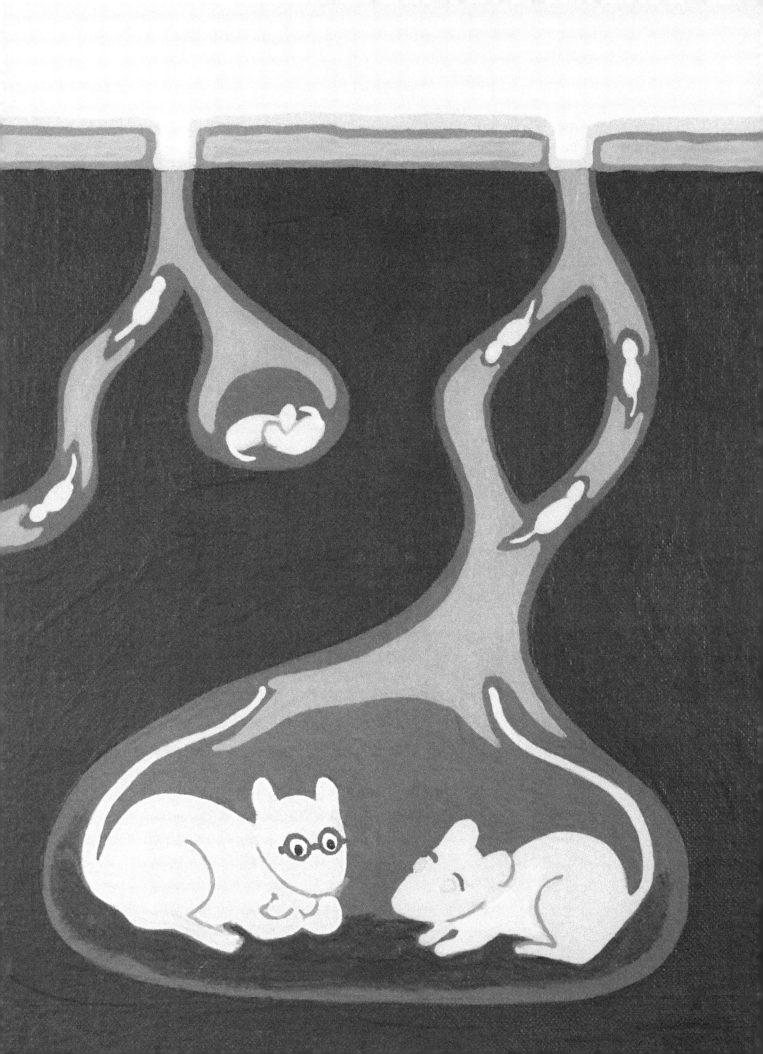

The second landed with a great splash,
but he didn't sink into the water's grasp.
He was floating inside a giant shell,
with fins that glided through the waters quite well.

A fish asked, "Why are your eyes so blue?
I have never seen a turtle quite like you."
"I'm cursed by the Dark Star and here's what's worse—
I have to find my brothers to break the curse."

"The Dark Star," continued the turtle, "cast a spell on us all.
Plucked us from the sky, watched us fall."
The fish replied, "Seek eyes of piercing blue,
and you will find brothers one and two."

The third landed near the bottom of the sea.

He was massive in size and felt quite angry.

In his mouth he could feel razor sharp teeth,

and he found himself glaring at the fish swimming beneath.

None of the sea creatures dared to remark

or venture too close to the blue-eyed shark.

He was grumpy and sullen, and felt quite alone.

He missed his brothers, and he missed his home.

Celestia the Queen kept her eye on the brothers,
knowing she would need great help from the others.
Mother Nature, the sun, the moon, and the wind
would all play a part to bring the curse to an end.

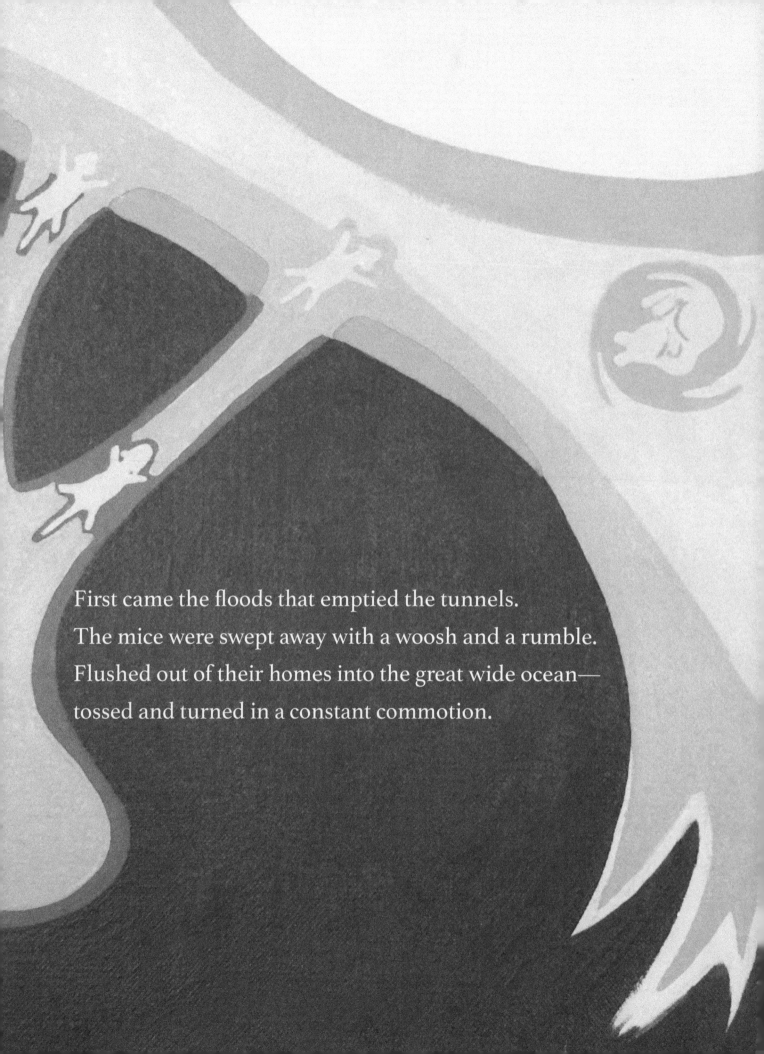

First came the floods that emptied the tunnels.
The mice were swept away with a woosh and a rumble.
Flushed out of their homes into the great wide ocean—
tossed and turned in a constant commotion.

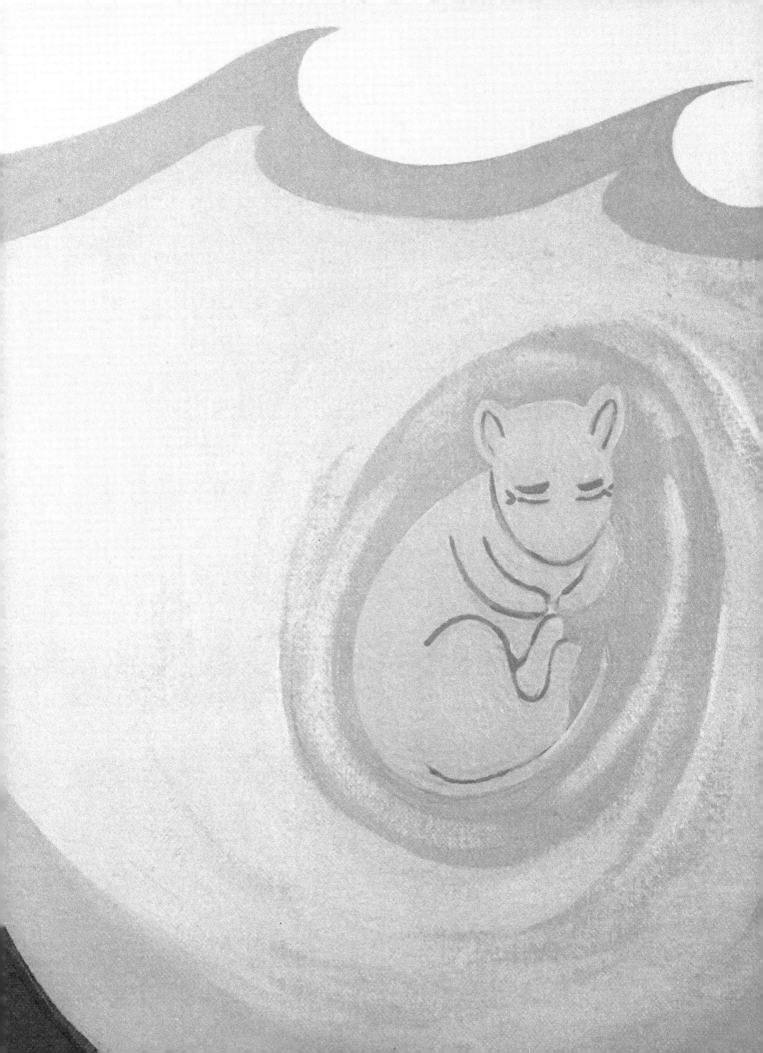

The blue-eyed mouse slammed into a rock.
It stunned him but he survived the shock.
He climbed on top and held on tight,
hoping he would make it through the night.

The impact woke the turtle sleeping inside.
He was sure that it was more than the shifting tide.
"I must go out and see what has rattled my shell.
Until now it has been a peaceful place to dwell."

There was a sudden shift and then out he came.
The blue-eyed turtle saw eyes that were the same.
Blue tears were shed at the glorious sight,
brother had found brother on this stormy night.

"Come inside brother—be safe and warm,
as we hunker down to ride out this storm.
We will begin our search when the storm has passed
and find our lost brother to break this spell at last."

It was some time before the travelers surfaced,
happy for the company, focused on their purpose.
The wind blew the shell to an ocean far away,
where the sea was calm and as clear as day.

The turtle and mouse poked out of the shell,
pleased to see no additional swells.
A dolphin was shocked to see the two
with identical eyes of sparkling blue.

"Have you heard of the shark that lives in these parts?
He's not a hunter, he has a kind heart.
But," said the dolphin, "what is strange but true—
his eyes are the same hue of blue as you two."

The brothers' joy knew no bounds
as they asked the dolphin where the shark could be found.
The dolphin replied, "At the bottom of the sea,
he keeps to himself by the coral reef."

The mouse slipped onto the dolphin's nose,
and as for the turtle, down he dove.
He found the shark with eyes of blue
and brought him up to the surface in full view.

Their heartfelt reunion was like no other,
for through some miracle brother had found brother;
miles away and through raging storms,
with different sizes, shapes, and forms.

The Dark Star looked on, not angered by their reunion.
Imagine his shock, imagine his confusion.
Overcome by feelings he hadn't felt for some time,
his heart was full, he regretted his crime.

The darkness drained from him in the shimmering moonlight,
and became a golden powder that rained down through the night.
"Stardust!" the brothers cried with twinkling eyes,
as the magic powder came down from the sky.

The turtle changed first, with a golden entourage.
He floated to the heavens and shed his camouflage.
Next, the shark became bathed in gold—
he shot up to the sky for all to behold.

Last was the mouse and the spell was no more;
he took his place, more brilliant than before.

They say the heavens never glistened as bright
as when the brothers returned home that night;
celestial warriors beaming with pride,
brother to brother, side by side.

CPSIA information can be obtained
at www.ICGtesting.com
Printed in the USA
BVHW02*1703290818
525892BV00005B/8/P